"'Twas The Morning of Christmas"

(An Adaptation of "Twas The Night Before Christmas")

By Mrs. Kathy L. Puder

First, I would like to thank God for the idea of this book, I would also like to thank my Husband, and my mom and my three children; Jackie, Codie, and Sydney, who inspires me and brings joy to my life each day. I love you with all my heart.

IT WAS THE MORNING OF CHRISTMAS
AND THROUGHOUT SANTA'S HOUSE
NO ONE WAS STIRRING
NOT EVEN SANTA'S SPOUSE!

THE CLAUS' STOCKINGS WERE HUNG
BY THE CHIMNEY WITH CARE
I COULDN'T IMAGINE THEM
NOT HANGING THERE!

SANTA WAS ALREADY NESTLED ALL SNUG IN HIS BED,
WHILE VISIONS OF CHRISTMAS COOKIES
DANCED IN HIS HEAD.
MRS. CLAUS HAD HER KERCHIEF
AND SANTA HAD HIS CAP
THEY HAD JUST SETTLED DOWN
FOR A CHRISTMAS MORNING NAP

THEN OUT ON THE LAWN
THERE AROSE SUCH CHATTER
MRS. CLAUS SPRANG FROM HER BED
TO SEE WHAT WAS THE MATTER.

AWAY TO THE WINDOW SHE FLEW
LIKE A FLASH,
SHE TORE OPEN THEIR SHUTTERS
AND THREW UP THEIR SASH.

THE SUN, TO THE EAST, SHOWED THE NEWLY -TRAMPLED SNOW
AND GAVE LIGHT FOR MRS.CLAUS TO LOOK DOWN BELOW,
WHEN WHAT BEFORE HER SLEEPY EYES SHOULD APPEAR,
BUT MINIATURE ELVES AND EIGHT TINY REINDEER;

KNOWING THE LITTLE OLD DRIVER
WAS SLEEPING LIKE A BRICK,
MRS. CLAUS KNEW IN A MOMENT
SHE MUST MOVE QUICK.
MORE RAPID THAN EAGLES
DOWN THE STAIRS SHE CAME,
AND SHE WHISPERED, BUT FIRMLY,
CALLED THEM BY NAME:

NOW DASHER! NOW DANCER!
NOW PRANCER! AND VIXEN!
COME ON, COMET! CUPID!
DONDER AND BLITZEN!
YOU ELVES TO THE PORCH
BE CAREFUL NOT TO FALL!
NOW DASH QUICKLY! DASH QUIETLY!
WHAT IS WITH YOU ALL?

SO TO THE PORCH THE ELVES
PUSHED THEIR WAY THROUGH
TO SHARE WITH MRS. CLAUS
WHAT THEY WERE ABOUT TO DO

THEN UP TO THE HOUSETOP
QUIETLY THEY FLEW,
WITH THE SLEIGH FULL OF GOODIES
FOR YOU-KNOW-WHO.

THEN IN A INSTANT, MRS. CLAUS
LISTENED FOR SOUNDS FROM THE ROOF
BUT HEARD NO PRANCING AND PAWING
FROM ANY LITTLE HOOF;

RELIEVED, SHE DREW IN HER HEAD
AND WAS TURNING AROUND,
WHEN DOWN THE CHIMNEY THE ELVES
CAME-MINUS THE BOUND.

DRESSED ALL IN ELF SUITS,
FROM EACH HEAD TO EACH FOOT,
YES, THEIR SUITS WERE ALL TARNISHED
WITH ASHES AND SOOT.

A BUNDLE OF GIFTS THEY HAD TAKEN OFF
THEIR BACKS,
THEY LOOKED LIKE MERCHANTS
OPENING THEIR PACKS.

THEIR EYES, HOW THEY TWINKLED!
THEIR DIMPLES, HOW MERRY!
THEIR RED CHEEKS WERE LIKE POINSETTAS,
THEIR NOSES WERE ROUND LIKE BERRIES!

THEY HAD DROLL LITTLE MOUTHS
DRAWN UP LIKE LITTLE BOWS,
SOME HAD BEARDS ON THEIR CHINS
THAT WERE WHITE LIKE THE SNOW;

THEY HAD ROUND FACES
TO MATCH THEIR ROUND BELLIES
THAT SHOOK, WHEN THEY LAUGHED,
LIKE BOWLS FULL OF JELLY.

THEY WERE CHUBBY AND PLUMP,
SPRITEFUL LITTLE ELVES,
MRS. CLAUS LAUGHED
WHEN SHE SAW THEM
QUIETLY TO HERSELF;

A WINK OF THEIR EYES,
AND A TWIST OF THEIR HEADS,
LET MRS. CLAUS KNOW
SHE HAD NOTHING TO DREAD;

THEY SPOKE NOT A WORD, BUT WENT
STRAIGHT TO THEIR WORK,
AND FILLED SANTA'S STOCKINGS,
USING AWESOME TEAMWORK,

AND LAYING A FINGER
ASIDE EACH LITTLE ROUND NOSE,
WITH LITTLE NODS, ONE AT A TIME,
UP THE CHIMNEY THEY AROSE;

THEY SPRANG TO SANTA'S SLEIGH,
AND TO HIS TEAM EACH GAVE A LOW WHISTLE,
AND AWAY TO THE STABLE THEY ALL FLEW
LIKE A WELL GUIDED MIISSLE.

MRS. CLAUS HEARD THEM EXCLAIM AS THEY
DROVE OUT OF SIGHT,
"HAPPY CHRISTMAS MORNING TO ALL AND
TO ALL SLEEP TIGHT."

Made in the USA
Charleston, SC
20 November 2015